HarperFestival is an imprint of HarperCollins Publishers.

The Angry Birds™ Movie Official Guidebook
© 2016 Rovio Animation Ltd., Angry Birds, and all related properties, titles, logos, and characters are
trademarks of Rovio Entertainment Ltd. and Rovio Animation Ltd. and are used with permission.
All rights reserved. Printed in the United States of America.
No part of this book may be used or reproduced in any manner whatsoever without written permission
except in the case of brief quotations embodied in critical articles and reviews. For information address
HarperCollins Children's Books, a division of HarperCollins Publishers, 195 Broadway, New York, NY 10007.
www.harpercollinschildrens.com

Library of Congress Control Number: 2015954738
ISBN 978-0-06-245342-6

Book design by Robert Steimle and Victor Joseph Ochoa
16 17 18 19 20 PC/RRDC 10 9 8 7 6 5 4 3 2 1
❖
First Edition

Concept Art by:
Pete Oswald (12–13, 16–17, 20–21),
Erwin Madrid (20–21),
Jeanie Chang (22–23, 24–25, 26–27, 30–35,
40–41, 94–95, 118–119, 126–127, 148–149),
Travis Ruiz (24–25, 26–27, 28–29, 84–85, 88–89,
118–119, 122–123, 134–139, 152–153),
Sue Blanchard (24–25),
John Nevarez (28–29, 50–51, 126–127),
Samantha Kalis (50–51, 151),
Fernando Cintra (88–89),
Ernie Rinard (61, 140–145, 151),
Aaron Spurgeon (122–123),
Alger Tam (140–145, 154–155),
Yashar Tahtolkassai (122–125, 134–139, 147),
Sharon Huang (124–125, 154–155)

THE ANGRY BIRDS™ MOVIE

OFFICIAL GUIDEBOOK

BY CHRIS CERASI

HARPER FESTIVAL
An Imprint of HarperCollinsPublishers

THE BIRDS OF BIRD ISLAND: A QUICK HELLO!

Welcome! This handy introduction will help you familiarize yourself with the friendly feathered folks who live here. Your guide will be with you shortly.

BE HAPPY

WELCOME ANGRY BIRDS TODAY

Bomb

Bubbles

Chuck

Cyrus

Edward

Eva

Hal

Judge Peckinpah

Matilda

Mighty Eagle

Red

Shirley

Stella

Terence

Timothy

CONTENTS

SECTION 1

99% ANGRY

O h, ah. Hi there. Um, so... My name is Red. I'm apparently an "angry bird," but if you ask me, everyone else is so dang cheerful all the time that anything less than a beak-splitting grin is considered angry! Anyway, as part of my anger-management training, I've been asked to be your guide through Bird Island. Normally that pink bundle of annoying energy named Stella would be your guide, but I don't have much of a choice. So let's just get this over with so I can go back to being with my favorite person (myself) and doing what I love best (which—you guessed it—is being left alone!).

But before we get started, please just keep one thing in mind. Think of this as one of Red's Rules: *Some birds are born to be angry.*

So, uh, yeah, welcome to the world of the Angry Birds. Try not to ask too many questions, okay?

WELCOME TO
BIRD ISLAND

Bird Island is in the middle of a vast sea. It's a big place, full of dense jungles, large mountains, sandy beaches, waterfalls, green forests, and rocky cliffs. It has every environment a bird could want, plus the weather is almost always sunny and nice. Don't tell Stella I said this, but it's pretty much the most

JUNGLE

BEACH

beautiful place I have ever lived. It's also the *only* place I have ever lived, but, whatever. It's my home, and it's the best home a bird could ask for.

I live on the island with—you guessed it—my fellow birds. I'm supposed to say that we're a happy, carefree bunch, and that's basically true of almost every bird. I'm not unhappy, mind you. I'm just not particularly all-the-time-happy. But at the end of the day, I really am glad I live in such a beautiful place. Here's a map with a few special spots labeled, in case you want to explore.

See, that was almost cheerful, wasn't it?

MIGHTY EAGLE'S SECRET
MOUNTAIN LAIR
—APPROXIMATE LOCATION
(YOU KNOW WHAT A *SECRET* IS, RIGHT?)

FOREST

BIRD VILLAGE

RED

I guess I should tell you a little about myself. Normally I am a very private bird, but since I had to take anger-management classes, I don't have much of a choice. Here's a test I took during class. A lot of birds have taken it—for fun. It's supposed to help us get in touch with our inner songbirds. Whatever. Here are my answers.

ALL ABOUT RED

OCCUPATION: Wanting to be left alone!

FAVORITE COLOR: Red, duh.

FAVORITE BOOK: Any Mighty Eagle comic book that I can read by myself in my own hut, thankyouverymuch!

SPECIAL SKILLS: I am very good at spending time ALONE.

HOBBIES: Being alone. Pretty much doing anything alone.

FAVORITE PLACE ON BIRD ISLAND: My own hut.

BEST FRIEND: Me. Well, I guess Chuck is pretty cool. And Bomb. But don't tell them I said so.

GREATEST WISH: To be left alone.

BIGGEST FEAR: Being hugged.

WHAT MAKES YOU HAPPY? Privacy.

WHAT MAKES YOU ANGRY? Being asked all these questions! And slow-moving birds. And loud birds. And late birds. And spoiled birds. And cheerful birds. And birds who stand too close. And birds who complain. And cheerful birds. And that bird who likes to give hugs. And birds who don't respect personal space. And birds who make me do anger management. And cheerful birds. Oh, and did I mention birds who are so dang cheerful that it starts TO MAKE ME ANGRY, and also EVERY BIRD AND THING AND PLACE ON THIS ISLAND?!

MOTTO: Keep to yourself. It's better that way.

A Great Way to Start Your Day

My hut is on the beach, far away from everyone else's (which is how I like it), so the paper delivery almost always comes later in the morning, which tends to make me a bit angry. But if I wanted my paper earlier, I'd have to live closer to the other birds, which is definitely NOT going to happen. *The Daily Peep* is the only newspaper on Bird Island. Take a gander and see if there are any island events you want to attend (or avoid). *The Daily Peep* is pretty informative, even though I've been featured in it a few times, and they've made me out to be some sort of recluse with a bad attitude.

Anyway, breakfast and *The Daily Peep* are how I start my day. Then I work on my plans for my dream hut—something even bigger and more private than the one I am currently living in.

You're on island time now, so do like I do: ease into the day.

Dream nest model

Calming ocean view

Indoor/outdoor bath for private bathing

Stairs to my personal sanctuary

17

The Daily Peep

Raving Red Battles Boisterous Beach Birds

A certain red bird runs the risk of becoming Bird Island's resident party pooper as his foul temper ruins another bird-day party days after the first, now-infamous Bird-Day Blow-Up.

Sources say that Red, a resident of Bird Island Beach, became enraged when noise from a nearby bird-day celebration grew too loud and disturbed his privacy and peace. It is unclear when the party-goers arrived and began their festivities, but appar-

ently they were partying too closely and too loudly for Red's comfort. And as each errant beach ball bounced against Red's hut, his anger escalated.

An anonymous witness says the final blow—a beach ball to the head—set off Red's spectacular temper explosion. He began kicking sand everywhere and squawking loudly about his space being invaded.

"It was terrible," said one of the party attendees. "Red just came running out of his house and began yelling. All we were doing was celebrating my friend Gus's twelfth bird-day with cake, games, and a few noisemakers. He just turned into a red orb of anger! The way he screamed at us and carried on, you would think we had tossed fireworks inside his hut." When pressed, this partygoer admitted that quite a few beach balls had ricocheted off of Red's home and that the partyers may have targeted the hut once the recluse started confiscating the inflatable objects.

When reached for comment, Red refused to leave his house and would only shout "Go away!" behind his closed door. It is unclear if this latest outburst will impact the terms of Red's court-sanctioned anger-management classes. But all of Bird Island hopes that one day soon this extremely angry bird will change his ways.

BIRD VILLAGE

Almost all the birds of Bird Island live in the area known as Bird Village. This is where many birds work, shop, relax, eat, and do just about everything else. Main Street runs right through the middle of the village. It's the epicenter of bird culture and life. Because this is

where everything is happening, it's also a popular place to hang out. So you *might* run into me in town. It would be better if there weren't so many other birds around and *so* much better if only the birds I liked lived there. But I guess it takes more than three birds to make a village.

DOWN ON MAIN STREET

Bird Village has a lot of interesting shops and businesses. Even though I avoid these places, you'll probably enjoy making a few stops while strolling down Main Street. Here are a few standouts for food, fun, and learning about life on Bird Island.

EARLY BIRD WORMS

This is the best place to get the most delicious worms in the whole of Bird Village. The owner imports them from all over the island. Like the name says, you have to get here pretty early in the day to get the choicest worms. It means having to wait in a long line with some of the most annoying . . . uh, that is, *lively* birds in the village. Who tend to stand real close. So set your alarm clocks and get ready to fill a big bucket of the juiciest, finest worms. Then head to the park for a picnic.

LATE RISER WORMS

This is the worst place to get worms in the whole of Bird Village, unless you like your worms skinny, chewy, and stale. The bird who runs this shop is a heck of a bird. But he just gets up too late and ends up with all the rejected worms from the Early Bird! There's always a small line outside his shop, and it's usually made up of those birds who just can't seem to get their feathers together.

EARLY BIRD WORMS

LATE RISER WORMS

SORRY NO WORMS TODAY

THE BIRD BATH

The Bird Bath is a must-see destination for most birds when it's warm and sunny—which is almost every day on Bird Island. Do you like to cool off while conversing with other birds, or splash around in style? Either way, be prepared for crowds at the hottest spot for chilling out.

THE BIRD BATH ENTRANCE

BIRD DAY CARE CENTER

This is a place I usually walk by as fast as I can. You have to be . . . well, everything I'm not in order to work there! Patient, understanding, nurturing . . . patient. Listen, I know my flaws, okay?

Still, for those who have children, this really is a great place to bring unhatched birdlings, as the birds here are "trained to take the very best care of your precious cargo, surrounding them with love, personal attention, and only positive energy."

Okay, I just read all of that from the brochure. So sue me.

HUG TRADER

Oh boy, *this guy*. He trades in hugs, just like his store name says. He stands outside his shop and gives hugs to any bird who looks slightly interested! Every time I walk by, he looks at me expecting a hug, and every time my answer is the same: nuh-uh! No way. NOT going to happen. Nope. No, no, and no.

NAP BAR

Who doesn't love a good nap at least once or twice a day? For the bird on the go, this is the best place to catch up on some much-needed rest. The hammocks are super-comfy, and the soft island breeze gently lulls you to sleep. Sweet dreams are guaranteed.

Birds of a Feather Salon

There are a lot of fashionable birds on Bird Island, and they all go to Birds of a Feather Salon to get their feathers done in style. Curled, dyed, streaked, teased, trimmed, fluffed, you name it. There is always a crowd there, and it's a constant flurry of activity. Birds talking, birds laughing, birds cooing with delight.

I'll be honest. I tried going there once and it really wasn't for me. I personally prefer to clip my own feathers, as that way I don't have to listen to any silly conversations or deal with any other . . . anything. But Chuck swears by them, so, go figure.

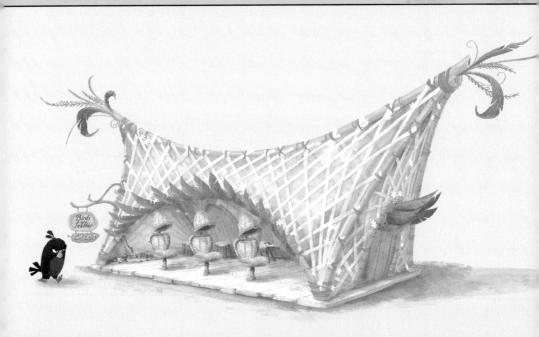

BIRDFEEDER RESTAURANT

Feathers-down, the Birdfeeder is the fanciest restaurant in Bird Village. It prides itself on locally sourcing the freshest ingredients from all over Bird Island. The fruit du jour is something to behold. And since the menu changes all the time, you're always in for a surprise. They put on great shows as well, so it's no wonder that you'll find a crowd there almost every night. The staff is also very accommodating. They always find a table for one if a bird happens to be flying solo.

BIRD ISLAND POLICE STATION

Even though you'll likely never have to go to the police station, it's worth knowing about—just in case you are an eyewitness to a minor altercation between a few rowdy partygoers and an innocent-until-proven-guilty beach-comber. So stop by for a quick "hello" when you're in the village.

THE WEEKLY BIRD ISLAND POLICE BLOTTER

Angry outburst in the diner–
subject and bystanders questioned

Angry outburst at the movies–
subject and bystanders questioned

Speeding ticket–
ticket issued

Unexplained detonation in the park–
bystanders questioned, still under investigation

Angry outburst at the beach–
subject and bystanders questioned

BIRD COURT

Bird Court is the source of justice and law and rules and all that . . . stuff. It is presided over by Judge Peckinpah, whose alleged wisdom and judgment keep Bird Island safe and secure. So he claims. All the time!

You can attend hearings anytime. And all birds must serve jury duty, so every chirp is heard and counted. Clearly something is working, since the island is such a peaceful place—most of the time for most of the birds. It's just difficult for birds who are repeat "guests" of the court to feel peaceful—*especially* if they are sentenced to anger-management classes.

But everyone agrees on one thing: the statue of Mighty Eagle that looms large in the background is a real shot in the wing. Mighty Eagle watches over all of Bird Island. His bravery and nobility are legendary. Just looking up at the majestic statue can soothe and inspire the angriest of birds.

Infinity Acceptance Center

Last we come to the bane of my existence—I mean, one of Bird Village's most fascinating places: the Infinity Acceptance Center, run by former Angry Bird Matilda. Everyone is welcome, especially those found to be a little too angry or stressed or antisocial. Attendees are forced—I mean *encouraged*—to discover inner peace and become better birds. A recovered Angry Bird, Matilda is now the foremost authority on what it means to be the most ideal bird. Through yoga, meditation, and painting, birds strive to find ideal means of expression and . . . Oh geez, I just can't. . . . This is killing me. I don't know about you, but I'm exhausted. Let's call it a day for now, okay? I gotta get out of here.

Top 10 Things to Avoid on Bird Island

Here is a list of the ten things that currently get my feathers in a fluff!

1. **Bird Court:** It's where I found myself sentenced to anger-management classes after a perfectly reasonable misunderstanding between me and a family at a bird-day party. That Judge Peckinpah is a MONSTER, I tell you!

2. **Matilda's Anger-management Class:** Hippie-dippy Matilda loves to "reform" Angry Birds, but if you ask me, her yolk is all scrambled.

3. **Late Riser Worms:** If you snooze, you lose at this place. Sleep in and run the risk of having the most unsatisfying meal on the island.

4. **Bird Day Care Center:** Imagine having to take care of all those unhatched birdlings?! I shudder just thinking about it.

5. **Central Bird Park:** All those birds having fun and being loud all around you, spoiling your peace and quiet? NO THANK YOU!

6. BIRD DOCTOR: Going to the doctor is no fun, especially if it involves a busted beak or a sprained wing. I try to stay safe at all times so I never wind up there. Although the birds there DO take good care of us, so I guess I shouldn't grumble. Much.

7. HUG TRADER: What kind of deranged bird WANTS to give and get hugs all the time?! As far as I am concerned, that is NOT normal!

8. THE BIRDFEEDER RESTAURANT: But only when the early-bird special is being served. It may be good for business, but it's not good for a peaceful dining experience.

9. POLICE STATION: Not that there's much crime on Bird Island, but you want to stay on the good side of these official birds. Trust me.

10. BIRDS OF A FEATHER SALON: I like my feathers trimmed just so, but I cannot tell you how many times these nitwits have taken too much off the top! They also take forever because their beaks never stop flapping!

BIRDS AT WORK

Ever wonder where you would work if you lived on Bird Island? Answer the questions below to see what your dream job would be.

WHICH OF THE FOLLOWING SOUNDS LIKE THE MOST FUN TO YOU?

A Reading storybooks to lots of sweet baby hatchlings.
B Serving up creative juicy worm salads to hungry customers.
C Making sure everyone has a chance for a nice, long afternoon nap.
D Reporting on interesting stories from all over the city.
E Teaching birds how to be calm, creative, and centered.

WHAT DO YOU THINK SOUNDS THE MOST FUN TO WEAR TO WORK?

A A soft T-shirt, so you can sit and work in comfort.
B An apron to protect your feathers while you create food masterpieces.
C A stopwatch to time things precisely.
D A hat with a sign that says PRESS on it.
E A bracelet made of beads and string.

WHICH OF THE FOLLOWING CHALLENGES SOUNDS MOST APPEALING TO YOU?

A Helping to care for and shape the future generation.
B Getting in the kitchen and experimenting with lots of food items and recipes.
C Making sure everyone is rested, healthy, and content.
D Asking lots of questions and doing lots of investigating.
E Helping others control their anger and find inner peace.

WHO WOULD YOU WANT TO HAVE AS LOYAL CUSTOMERS?

A Unhatched birdlings warm and cozy in their shells.
B Hungry birds eager to try your latest food masterpiece.
C Sleepy birds who can't wait to curl up for a really nice, long nap.
D Avid readers who can't wait to read all the latest news.
E Angry and stressed-out birds who need guidance and calm.

WHAT IS YOUR FAVORITE TIME TO WORK?

A Mornings and afternoons only, while busy parents are at work.
B Breakfast, lunch, and dinner, as I love being in the kitchen!
C Late mornings and mid-afternoons only.
D Around the clock—the news never sleeps!
E In the morning after a nice, healthy breakfast.

So what's your Bird Island job?!

If you answered A to most of the questions, you are a caretaker at the Bird Day Care Center.
If you answered B to most of the questions, you are a chef at the Birdfeeder Restaurant.
If you answered C to most of the questions, you are an attendant at the Nap Bar.
If you answered D to most of the questions, you are a reporter for *The Daily Peep*.
If you answered E to most of the questions, you are an instructor at the Infinity Acceptance Center.

WINDING DOWN

A little quiet time at the beach (also known as *my home*) is the perfect antidote to a long day in the village. It is essential after spending too much time with other birds. My advice? End your day with some seaside rest and relaxation. Just don't expect any small talk—or any talk, for that matter—if you happen to see me there.

I usually take a towel and my latest issue of the Mighty Eagle comic book and lay out for a while. The only sounds are usually the waves lapping against the shore and the gentle hum of insects (which also make excellent snacks). Every once in a while I have to deal with younger birds playing on

LOCAL FLORA—GREAT SPOT FOR IMPROMPTU INSECT SNACKING

PRIVATE PROPERTY—STAY AWAY

the beach, but usually they know not to disturb me, or they suffer the consequences. I have about a dozen confiscated beach balls gathering dust in my hut. That'll teach them!

Mighty Eagle comic books are essential reading for any bird in the know. They showcase the adventures and heroics of *the* greatest bird ever: Mighty Eagle. Known throughout Bird Island as the bird who watches over us all from high atop his mountain, he is the bravest, smartest, strongest, wisest, most heroic bird there is, and every bird knows that they owe everything to Mighty Eagle. There's a reason why his giant statue is in the middle of our village square. It's important to honor this legend. I hope one day I can be half the bird he is.

EMPTY BEACH—OPERATIVE WORD: EMPTY; NO BEACH BALLS IN SIGHT

GENTLE WAVES—MUCH MORE CALMING THAN YOGA

POP QUIZ!
Island Life

I hope you've been paying attention, because I'm going to ask you all about island life. Don't make me look bad, okay, or I'll have to go to another one of Matilda's classes.

1. WHAT IS THE NAME OF MY FAVORITE CAFÉ?

2. WHO IS THE JUDGE THAT PRESIDES OVER BIRD COURT?

3. WHO IS THE GREATEST BIRD OF ALL TIME, DEFENDER OF BIRD ISLAND?

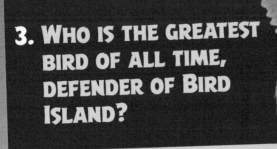

4. I GUESS I SORT-OF-KIND-OF-OKAY-YEAH HAVE TWO BEST FRIENDS. WHAT ARE THEIR NAMES?

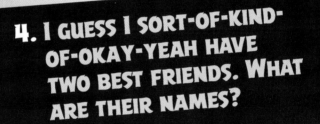

5. WHAT IS THE NAME OF BIRD ISLAND'S BEST (AND ONLY) NEWSPAPER?

6. Who runs the Infinity Acceptance Center (and is making my life MISERABLE)?

7. Where is the best place to get worms in Bird Village?

8. WHERE IS THE BEST PLACE TO GET YOUR FEATHERS TRIMMED?

9. TRUE OR FALSE:

I have lived in many places other than Bird Island.

10. TRUE OR FALSE:

The Hug Trader is my favorite place to go in Bird Village.

SECTION 2

MEET THE FLOCK

Sure Bird Island is beautiful and the shops are interesting. But the heart and soul of the island are—you guessed it—the birds. I either know them personally or have had, uh, dealings with them, but they are all essential parts of Bird Village. Ready for another one of Red's Rules? *Happy birds are too busy being happy to notice anything around them other than their own silly needs.* Do you want the happy? Can you handle the happy? Now is the time to find out.

JUDGE PECKINPAH

Judge Peckinpah loves three things most of all: the sound of his own voice, holding court—even when he's not actually in court—and sentencing birds to horrible things like daily anger-management classes at the Infinity Acceptance Center.

He can be seen strutting around Bird Village like he owns the place. The judge is so small that underneath his robes, he stands on the shoulders of another bird, Cyrus. But every bird knows the truth, so he's not fooling any of us. Judge Peckinpah believes he's answering a higher calling—one that requires a higher perch—on Cyrus's shoulders!

CYRUS

Cyrus, the judge's perch, has the worst job on Bird Island. If that isn't bad enough, he also suffers from terrible allergies, so he's constantly sneezing. Despite the daily dose of propping up Peckinpah and his never-ending allergies, Cyrus is extremely happy and carefree. I can't wrap my bird brain around that.

ALL ABOUT JUDGE PECKINPAH

OCCUPATION: Why, judge of Bird Court, of course.

FAVORITE COLOR: Brown, the color of my hammer and the symbol of justice!

FAVORITE BOOK: *The Basic Book of Bird Justice and Law*, Volumes 1–27. They are never far from my reach, since a few volumes make a good booster seat.

SPECIAL SKILLS: Dispensing the law, justice, authority, and equality all throughout the land!

HOBBIES: Judging. Golfing.

FAVORITE PLACE ON BIRD ISLAND: Bird Court, where else?

BEST FRIEND: Truth and justice. Oh, and I guess Cyrus, too.

GREATEST WISH: Justice for all.

BIGGEST FEAR: Being looked down upon by other birds.

WHAT MAKES YOU HAPPY? Dispensing the law, justice, authority, and equality all throughout the land!

WHAT MAKES YOU ANGRY? Disorder caused by Angry Birds.

MOTTO: Be the hammer of justice (or something just as heavy).

THE HALLOWED LAWS
OF BIRD ISLAND

1. Friendship and happiness always come first.

2. Every bird has the right to a safe, secure, and happy existence on Bird Island. Bad behavior will not be tolerated.

3. Every bird must treat one another and the environment with respect.

4. Rudeness and anger will not be tolerated.

5. Too many questions lead to disobedience and threaten the tranquility of Bird Island.

6. Respect your elders and other most learned of birds when frequenting stores and restaurants.

7. If bad behavior results in a trial, all birds are guaranteed a speedy public trial by a jury of their flock.

8. Be happy. No matter what.

JUDGE PECKINPAH'S ALL-TIME FAVORITE JOKES

Judge Peckinpah takes his job seriously. But outside of the court he has been known to tell a few jokes (some of them over and over again). Here are a few of his tired-and-true, that is, tried-and-true rib ticklers.

WHY DON'T BIRDS FLY?

WHY?

BECAUSE WHERE ELSE WOULD WE EVER WANT TO GO?

WHY COULDN'T THE FLOWER RIDE HER BIKE?

WHY?

BECAUSE SHE LOST HER PETALS!

KNOCK-KNOCK.

WHO'S THERE?

ORANGE.

ORANGE WHO?

ORANGE YOU GLAD I'M THE JUDGE?!

WHY DID THE BIRD CROSS THE ROAD?

WHY?

TO GET TO THE OTHER SIDE!

WHY DID THE WORM
CROSS THE ROAD?

WHY?

BECAUSE IT WAS THE
BIRD'S DAY OFF!

STELLA

Stella is one of the happiest and most optimistic birds around. Her pink feathers and constant smile make her popular with *almost* everyone. Occasionally her perky behavior ruffles some birds' feathers. She is an expert about everything on Bird Island and is proud of the island's history. Stella loves leading tours of the island, but is happy to hand over the reins if someone needs to fulfill an anger-management assignment.

ALL ABOUT STELLA

OCCUPATION: Official tour guide for Bird Island!

FAVORITE COLOR: Pink!

FAVORITE BOOK: *101 Parkour Moves*.

SPECIAL SKILLS: Parkour and Bird Island expert.

HOBBIES: Giving amazing tours, hanging out with my friends, and practicing my parkour moves!

FAVORITE PLACE ON BIRD ISLAND: Everywhere! I just LOVE this island!

BEST FRIEND: I'm BFFs with everyone!

GREATEST WISH: Happiness for every bird all the time!

BIGGEST FEAR: Unhappiness. And bad-feather days.

WHAT MAKES YOU HAPPY? Just about everything, but especially spending time with my friends and giving tours of Bird Island!

WHAT MAKES YOU ANGRY? Oh I never get angry, silly!

MOTTO: Hug today just like you hugged yesterday!

Dear Red,

I'm so happy you are giving a tour! You will love it! I can tell there's a stellar tour guide inside you just waiting to burst out.

Since I've been doing this for a long time, I thought you'd be interested in some super-fun hints and helpful suggestions. I've attached them here for you and will follow up soon to see if you have any questions—and to set up a time for the slide show!

Fondly,
Stella

P.S. Call me with any questions at all—day or night! I'm always happy to talk about the island.

The Week Before the Tour

Brush up on your island history.
Stop by my nest to watch my "Bird Island 101" slide show. It should take an hour to see all the slides. Maybe two hours. Wait, I've just updated it, so let's say three hours. Tops.

Stretch your feathers at a yoga class.
All that walking and pointing on the tour can leave you with some sore feathers.

The Night Before
Call me.
I'm always learning new facts about the island and will share the latest scoop.

Go to bed early.
There's nothing worse than tossing and turning in your nest all night.

The Big Day
Get excited!
You're about to turn your tour attendees into island experts. How thrilling is that?!

Bring something cool to drink.
All that talking will give you a parched beak.

Stop and smell the flowers.
Nothing smells as sweet as Bird Island flowers. Your tour will thank you for the nature break. And if you're lucky, you can sneak in a quick insect snack.

Most important, have F-U-N.

SHIRLEY

Shirley is the oldest bird on the island. It takes her a long time to get around! She manages to always be out and about Bird Village, especially when other birds are in a hurry. If you help her cross the road, she'll likely share a story about the good old days.

ALL ABOUT SHIRLEY

OCCUPATION: Oh goodness, I am long retired.

FAVORITE COLOR: Yellow, I think. Or it could be light blue. I don't remember, dearie.

FAVORITE BOOK: *I Know Why the Caged Bird Sings* speaks to my heart.

SPECIAL SKILLS: Oh, these days I'm just happy making it across the street in less than an hour.

HOBBIES: Knitting, crocheting, watching daytime TV, shopping, and taking a nice stroll through the garden.

FAVORITE PLACE ON BIRD ISLAND: My hut has been home to me for many years, so I like it there best.

BEST FRIEND: Officer Beakins. He always helps me cross the road.

GREATEST WISH: A new set of wheels and maybe a horn for my walker.

BIGGEST FEAR: Not making it home for my favorite show, *The Bird and the Beautiful*.

WHAT MAKES YOU HAPPY? Oh, pretty much every day is worth celebrating.

WHAT MAKES YOU ANGRY? I'm too old and tired to be angry. My, what a question!

MOTTO: Help an old lady across the street, will you?

HAL

Hal is a bongo-playing bird about town. He occasionally helps out at Matilda's Infinity Acceptance Center. Hal's specialty is any class where a steady beat is needed. Hal is known as the "boomerang bird" due to his large beak.

ALL ABOUT HAL

OCCUPATION: Percussionist.

FAVORITE COLOR: Red-hot jazz.

FAVORITE BOOK: *The Tin Drum.*

SPECIAL SKILLS: Playing a duet. Soothing Angry Birds through music.

HOBBIES: Playing and writing music.

FAVORITE PLACE ON BIRD ISLAND: Anywhere I can play my bongos, which is pretty much anywhere.

BEST FRIEND: Bubbles.

GREATEST WISH: To form a marching band.

BIGGEST FEAR: Misplacing my bongo set.

WHAT MAKES YOU HAPPY? The beat of my heart synching up with the beat of my drum.

WHAT MAKES YOU ANGRY? Missing a beat.

MOTTO: March to the beat of your own drum. But if you don't have a drum, march to the beat of mine!

BUBBLES

If you hear the sweet sounds of a horn, chances are Bubbles is nearby. Like Hal, this popular island musician keeps the island birds entertained with the toot of his horn. He also lends his talents to the Infinity Acceptance Center. Bubbles does best in classes where calming sounds are needed. He can literally blow up to more than three times his normal size when he's excited or surprised, as the Hug Trader recently discovered. Talk about a big squeeze!

ALL ABOUT BUBBLES

OCCUPATION: Musician.

FAVORITE COLOR: The blues.

FAVORITE BOOK: Any book about music.

SPECIAL SKILLS: Improvising.

HOBBIES: Playing and listening to music.

FAVORITE PLACE ON BIRD ISLAND: The Birdfeeder— the acoustics are perfect there.

BEST FRIEND: Hal.

GREATEST WISH: To perform at Carn-egg-ie Hall.

BIGGEST FEAR: Hitting the wrong note during a big performance.

WHAT MAKES YOU HAPPY? Blowing the horn.

WHAT MAKES YOU ANGRY? Being out of tune.

MOTTO: A song a day keeps the blues away, unless you're playing rhythm and blues, then it's totally okay.

TERENCE

Terence is a bird of very few words. In fact, Terence is a bird of pretty much NO words! He mostly growls and groans and sighs. He's the biggest, tallest bird on the island, and he also might be the scariest bird on the island as well. He's a permanent member of Matilda's anger-management class due to an unspecified classified incident. His art therapy samples show signs of a true artistic calling. But there's no indication of Terence answering that call, since he doesn't speak! Underneath all that bulk and brawn, many suspect that Terence is really just a big softie.

ALL ABOUT TERENCE

OCCUPATION: Grrrr.

FAVORITE COLOR: Hnnnn.

FAVORITE BOOK: Grrrr.

SPECIAL SKILLS: Hnnnn.

HOBBIES: Grrrr.

FAVORITE PLACE ON BIRD ISLAND: Hnnnn.

BEST FRIEND: Grrrr.

GREATEST WISH: Hnnnn.

BIGGEST FEAR: Grrrr.

WHAT MAKES YOU HAPPY? Hnnnn.

WHAT MAKES YOU ANGRY? Grrrr.

MOTTO: Hnnnn.

FAMILY TIES

Families are a big deal on Bird Island. *Almost* everyone has one, is hatching one, or is thinking about hatching one. I don't have a whole lot of experience with families, but a recent encounter with a particular—and I do mean particular—family sticks in my mind.

Meet dad, Edward, mom, Eva, and son, Timothy. They are your typical family. They treat bird-days like national holidays and are very finicky about food. Being punctual is *really* important to them as well. Spending every waking moment together is also a really big deal. It's definitely not my scene.

ALL ABOUT EVA

OCCUPATION: Being a mom. It's a full-time job.

FAVORITE COLOR: Baby blue.

FAVORITE BOOK: Any book we can read together as a family.

SPECIAL SKILLS: Raising perfect hatchlings.

HOBBIES: Hobbies? Who has time for hobbies?

FAVORITE PLACE ON BIRD ISLAND: Our nest, sweet nest.

BEST FRIEND: My family. And other moms with new hatchlings.

GREATEST WISH: To travel back in time and hire anyone but Red as the entertainment at Timothy's bird-day party.

BIGGEST FEAR: Clowns.

WHAT MAKES YOU HAPPY? Family time.

WHAT MAKES YOU ANGRY? Late Angry Birds.

MOTTO: Our nest is best!

MIGHTY EAGLE

Mighty Eagle is the stuff of legends. Heck, he IS a legend! Heroic, brave, adventurous, and strong, Mighty Eagle watches over Bird Island and makes sure no harm comes to the birds. He is the subject of songs, poems, comic books, stories, and even fan fiction. He represents the very best of birdkind. Rumor has it that he can even fly!

Mighty Eagle lives far above us all in his mountaintop aerie in the Ancient Tree by the Lake of Wisdom. He is rarely seen in public, but islanders sense his presence and are reassured by his far-reaching greatness. His intelligence and bravery are inspiring, and every bird aims to be noble and good like this legendary hero.

ALL ABOUT MIGHTY EAGLE

OCCUPATION: Hero and protector. Defender of homes and liberty!

FAVORITE COLOR: Clear blue, the color of the sky from my mountaintop.

FAVORITE BOOK: *Mighty Eagle's Book of Wisdom.*

SPECIAL SKILLS: Bravery, strength, heroism, humility, and flying.

HOBBIES: Telling stories of the magnificent past.

FAVORITE PLACE ON BIRD ISLAND: My cave (aka the Hall of Heroism).

BEST FRIEND: No one. A hero must stand alone.

GREATEST WISH: That all of Bird Island sings my praises.

BIGGEST FEAR: None. I am fearless.

WHAT MAKES YOU HAPPY? Being strong.

WHAT MAKES YOU ANGRY? Nothing. I am too brave to be angry.

MOTTO: Mighty Eagle flying free, defender of homes and liberty!

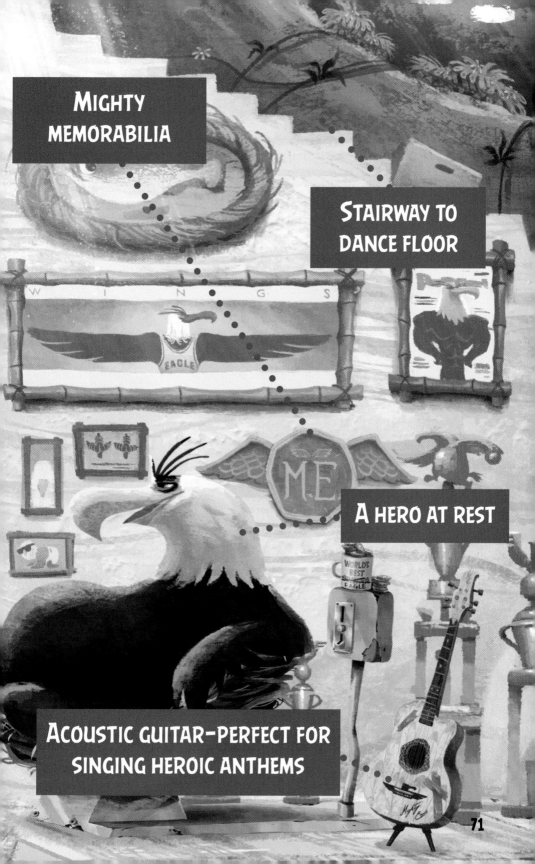

MIGHTY MEMORABILIA

STAIRWAY TO DANCE FLOOR

A HERO AT REST

ACOUSTIC GUITAR-PERFECT FOR SINGING HEROIC ANTHEMS

FACT OR FICTION:
THE LEGEND OF MIGHTY EAGLE

I consider myself the top authority on Mighty Eagle. I've studied his comics inside and out and backward and forward. Instead of one of Matilda's annoying quizzes, here's one that's a *lot more fun*. See if you can separate the fact from the fiction when it comes to Mighty Eagle.

1. TRUE OR FALSE:
Mighty Eagle can fly.

2. TRUE OR FALSE:
Mighty Eagle is the real author and illustrator of the Mighty Eagle comic book series. He writes with a feathered quill—plucked from his own wing.

3. TRUE OR FALSE:

Mighty Eagle was the lead singer in a rock 'n' roll band.

4. TRUE OR FALSE:

Mighty Eagle started the dance crazy known as "the Bustle."

5. TRUE OR FALSE:

Mighty Eagle owns a company that sells sardines.

6. TRUE OR FALSE:

Mighty Eagle is 1/64 Pegasus.

7. TRUE OR FALSE:

Mighty Eagle invented the ice cream flavors Butter Peckan and Chocolate Chirp.

8. TRUE OR FALSE:

Mighty Eagle's favorite food is coconut.

Pop Quiz!

Birdsonality Test

Ever wonder which member of the flock you are most similar to? Answer the questions below, then see what your matching birdsonality would be. Ask each of your friends these fun questions and see which bird they wind up with!

WHICH OF THE FOLLOWING SOUNDS MOST LIKE YOU?

A I'm always excited and happy at the start of each day!

B I cannot wait to start talking to anyone who'll listen.

C I wake up each day hoping there is nothing that puts me in a bad mood.

D I don't like to be talked to first thing in the morning.

E I can't wait to show everyone how brave and strong I am!

WHAT ARE THE TYPES OF FRIENDS YOU LIKE TO HAVE AROUND YOU?

A Super-fun and adventurous people!

B Those who will listen to what I have to say and appreciate my wisdom.

C I'm really more of a loner.

D Those who are just a little intimidated by my air of mystery.

E Those who are impressed with physical feats!

WHAT IS YOUR BEST QUALITY?

A I like to stay positive, no matter what!

B My wisdom and judgment.

C I'm the only one who thinks the way I do.

D My silence.

E My bravery, physical skills, and heroism.

WHAT TYPES OF THINGS WOULD YOU DO IF YOU THREW A PARTY?

A Games and activities that involve everyone and have us all laughing!

B Let everyone hear stories and poems I have written specially for the occasion.

C I probably wouldn't plan a party anytime soon.

D I'd leave planning things up to someone else.

E Lots of games and activities that require physical skills, especially dancing!

WHAT DO YOU THINK SOUNDS LIKE THE MOST FUN THING TO DO?

A Discover new places and explore with my best friends!

B Listen to friends' problems and give what I think is the best advice.

C Spend some quality time alone with a good book.

D Pick flowers in the park.

E Challenge myself with fun exercises and physical games.

SO WHAT'S YOUR BIRDSONALITY?!

If you answered **A** to most of the questions, you are most like Stella.

If you answered **B** to most of the questions, you are most like Judge Peckinpah.

If you answered **C** to most of the questions, you are most like Red.

If you answered **D** to most of the questions, you are most like Terence.

If you answered **E** to most of the questions, you are most like Mighty Eagle.

SECTION

3

THEY'RE NOT MAD, THEY'RE ANGRY

While the majority of Bird Island residents are happy twenty-four hours a day, seven days a week, there is a small segment of the population that is angry. Very angry. It usually feels like the birdiverse is against them. But one time, the stars lined up perfectly and I found myself forced to spend time with a few other Angry Birds in an anger-management class. Which leads me to another of Red's Rules: *when life gives you anger-management classes, make yourself angrier.*

CHUCK

Chuck is one of the most animated birds on the island. He has more energy and speed than any other bird. And when they go unchecked, he can be very volatile. Still, his heart is in the right place, and he wants to be everyone's friend—even birds who aren't looking for a friend. He walks, talks, runs, eats, reads, sleeps, and even *thinks* fast! Chuck gets bored easily and ended up in anger-management classes after a few too many speeding tickets.

ALL ABOUT CHUCK

OCCUPATION: What does this mean?

FAVORITE COLOR: Yellow! But I also like red. And brown. And black. And green. And orange and pink and lots of other colors!

FAVORITE BOOK: But there are 50 many! Right now I'm speed-reading a running manual, a crime novel, a biography of Mighty Eagle, and the *Complete Encyclopedia of Tropical Birds*!

SPECIAL SKILLS: I can run and move and talk faster than any other bird on Bird Island!

HOBBIES: Running, dancing, jumping, singing, hopping, skipping, fencing, spinning, and twirling! And I like to knit, too. You know, for quiet time.

FAVORITE PLACE ON BIRD ISLAND: My house! Oh, and Bomb's house, the Infinity Acceptance Center, the Birdfeeder Restaurant . . . pretty much everywhere and anywhere on the island!

BEST FRIEND: Bomb and Red! And I guess Matilda, too, although I wouldn't say she's my best friend. More like a friendly instructor. But I love having friends! Friends, friends, friends!

GREATEST WISH: To run wherever I want. And to sing and dance and have everyone come to my shows that will undoubtedly be huge hits!

BIGGEST FEAR: Having to sit still.

WHAT MAKES YOU HAPPY? Pretty much everything, but especially running and being fast! And a really good seed-and-worm sundae. Ooh, now I want ice cream!

WHAT MAKES YOU ANGRY? I definitely do not like getting speeding tickets, especially three tickets in one day. That is NOT fun. I also don't like slow-moving birds, slow eaters, birds who are late, or any bird who insults Mighty Eagle!

MOTTO: Keep moving! Or run like the wind! Ooh, I could probably think up some others. . . .

WORKING OUT WITH CHUCK

Whether it's running, dancing, walking, or spinning, Chuck likes to move, move, move! The whole island is his playground. But not every bird is like him. That's why he's come up with some simple steps to get the most out of working out.

1 **ALWAYS HAVE A GOOD SNACK BEFORE EXERCISING:** This is really important, as your body needs fuel before you work out. Chuck typically drinks a good seedshake before exercising.

2 **PICK A COMFORTABLE SPOT:** Exercising in a place that you like or that makes you feel relaxed is key to a good workout. No bird wants to exercise somewhere they don't like or that makes them feel tense.

3 **PACE YOURSELF:** Don't overdo it or push yourself too hard. You don't want to get hurt or do more harm than good. So know your limits. Start slow and then work your way to faster and longer exercises. Even though Chuck loves to race, exercising isn't a race. The only one you need to impress is yourself!

4 **USE THE BUDDY SYSTEM:** Sometimes it's easier to exercise when you have a friend with you. And if you want to see how fast you run, you'll need someone to race against. (Chuck is always ready.)

5 **THE MOST IMPORTANT TIP OF ALL:** Keep the friendly competition fun. Exercising is a really great way to take care of yourself, but it is also good for your brain and your mood.

Chuck's Hut

When Chuck isn't racing around the island, he's a real homebody. He thought of everything when he designed his home. The only thing he'd add are friends. There's *always* room for friends at Casa Chuck.

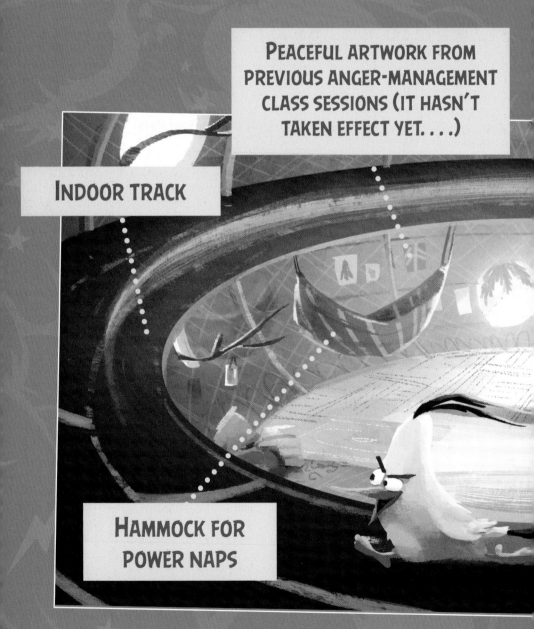

PEACEFUL ARTWORK FROM PREVIOUS ANGER-MANAGEMENT CLASS SESSIONS (IT HASN'T TAKEN EFFECT YET. . . .)

INDOOR TRACK

HAMMOCK FOR POWER NAPS

INDOOR TREE—PERFECT FOR PULL-UPS

BOMB

Bomb is the only bird with IED, or Intermittent Explosive Disorder. He can't control when or where he'll explode. Usually stress or being surprised triggers Bomb to detonate, but there have been plenty of times that he's exploded under more normal circumstances. Bomb has a big heart and is a gentle giant. He wouldn't hurt a fly. Well, he'd eat the fly, technically, but he wouldn't hurt it. If that makes sense.

ALL ABOUT BOMB

OCCUPATION: Yes.

FAVORITE COLOR: Black. No, blue! Or maybe red? I don't know. What do you think?

FAVORITE BOOK: Any book read out loud. Listening to other people read aloud helps me relax.

SPECIAL SKILLS: Exploding, but I'm still figuring out how to control it.

HOBBIES: Painting. Keeping up with Chuck.

FAVORITE PLACE ON BIRD ISLAND: Oh, I like Chuck's house. And mine is nice. And maybe the beach.

BEST FRIEND: Chuck is pretty great. And Red, too. Yeah. They're probably my best pals.

GREATEST WISH: To control my explosions.

BIGGEST FEAR: Surprise parties—there's usually a surprise that no one expects when I'm around—the ultimate party foul.

WHAT MAKES YOU HAPPY? Anger-management classes. They're fun!

WHAT MAKES YOU ANGRY? When other birds see me as just an explosive freak of nature. I have feelings, too!

MOTTO: Keep calm and carry a fire extinguisher.

BOMB'S HUT

SLIGHTLY CHARRED ROOF

CURTAINS DRAWN
—AN UNEXPECTED GUST OF WIND
COULD CAUSE AN IED INCIDENT

TRIGGER WARNINGS:
WHEN BOMB
GOES BOOM

Bomb doesn't let his IED hold him back. If you see him out and about, say hello. He's really a great guy. But it doesn't hurt to be aware that an unexpected *ka-boom!* may be lurking. Here are some situations he tries to avoid:

1 STRESS: Nothing makes Bomb go boom like too much stress. He blew the roof off the Infinity Acceptance Center twice during his first week of classes. Holding a tricky yoga pose or taking quizzes can cause stress for some people. I'm just saying.

2 SURPRISES: Don't sneak up on Bomb, or even do anything that can take him by surprise. He's not the kind of guy who can handle a surprise bird-day party, but he's great at planning a prank.

3 EXTREME HAPPINESS: You know how some birds say they could "explode with happiness"? Well, Bomb is the only bird who actually does that! Not only did he explode when everyone yelled "Surprise!" at his bird-day party, but he exploded later on when opening his gifts. Singed feathers was an unexpected "theme" that night.

4 ANGER: Bomb rarely gets so angry that he explodes. Once something big, really big happened. And the explosion was so immense that he landed in anger-management training classes.

5 SPONTANEOUS EXPLOSION: Because of his IED, Bomb can explode wherever and whenever, which makes his life much more . . . interesting. It's one of the reasons he doesn't have a lot of friends. And that's too bad since he is loyal and always up for an adventure. Plus, who doesn't want a little spontaneity in life, right?

MATILDA

Matilda runs the Infinity Acceptance Center, Bird Island's first and only place dedicated to promoting the well-being of birds everywhere. She's also the head instructor. She has a "Free Range" certificate, which means she's qualified to teach other birds how to be less angry and more peaceful, productive members of bird society. She is a former Angry Bird, so she's clucked the cluck and walked the walk. Her goal is for all birds to leave her classes happier, calmer, and more centered (with the exception of Red, but she's working on it!).

ALL ABOUT MATILDA

OCCUPATION: Instructor of the Infinity Acceptance Center!

FAVORITE COLOR: Every color has its own beauty and its own special magic.

FAVORITE BOOK: *The Seven Habits of Highly Effective Birds* is a very influential book for me.

SPECIAL SKILLS: Providing grounding, emotional support and nurturing talents in a nonjudgmental and personal way.

HOBBIES: Gardening, meditation, yoga, and being in nature.

FAVORITE PLACE ON BIRD ISLAND: The Infinity Acceptance Center, where every bird is welcome!

BEST FRIEND: The birdiverse is my best friend.

GREATEST WISH: To unite birdkind in an invisible web of love and light and happiness and peace!

BIGGEST FEAR: Not getting through to the birds who need me most, like Red. His anger is a daily challenge.

WHAT MAKES YOU HAPPY? Look around—what's not to love about Bird Island and our magnificent home?

WHAT MAKES YOU ANGRY? Those who refuse to listen or work toward their own happiness. It's very hard when a bird is unwilling to cooperate and deliberately makes things harder. I CAN'T STAND THAT! Oh my goodness! I lost my temper then. Breathe, Matilda, breathe. Quiet, mindful thoughts . . . There, that's better.

MOTTO: Every bird is beautiful!

INFINITY ACCEPTANCE CENTER

The Infinity Acceptance Center is Bird Island's only studio for stress reduction, anger management, and emotional well-being. This safe, nurturing, and cozy

ZEN GARDEN

REFLECTIVE POOL

space was created for the citizens of Bird Island after its founder, Matilda, was able to overcome her own anger issues. Realizing the self-destructive nature of lost tempers, short fuses, and explosive confrontations was the first step. After seeking help and learning to become a happier, calmer, and more peaceful bird, Matilda wanted to help others and the Infinity Acceptance Center was born.

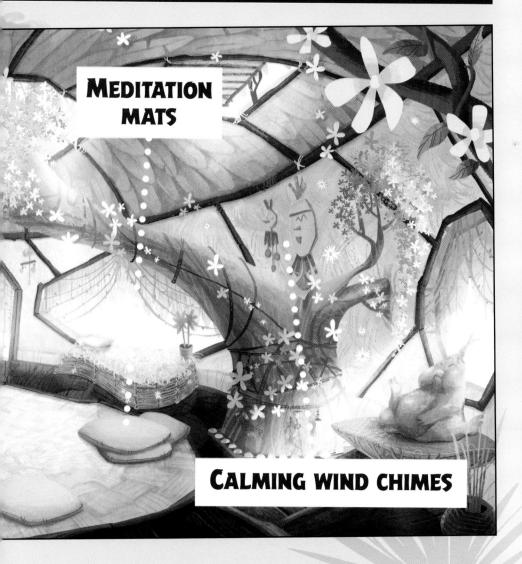

MEDITATION MATS

CALMING WIND CHIMES

IAC
Course Listings

The Infinity Acceptance Center offers a variety of courses from which to choose. Whether you're a bird on the go, curious about expanding your mind, or have been sentenced to attend classes here by the court, you'll find plenty of options to fit your needs and your time. Take a moment to browse our course listings, and sign up for those that interest you!

Mindful Meditation: Does it feel like you could explode at any moment? Does your mind race when running around the island? Have you spent a day at the beach kicking sand to keep others away? Then this is the class for you. Using just your imagination, discover you own mantra and learn how to incorporate it at home. To note: repeating phrases like "born to be angry" or "nice birds finish last" do not constitute mantras.

YOGA: Follow a simple series of poses to bring about peacefulness and relaxation. Important: students with Intermittent Explosive Disorder should see the instructor before class in order to identify IED triggers and learn modified poses.

PAINTING: Express your inner Michel-egg-elo through painting. From nature to still life to portraits and more, painting is a great way to express yourself. This is a judgment-free zone. All artists' work and works-in-progress will be respected.

ARTS AND CRAFTS: Get ready to transform everyday objects into art. Express yourself creatively through crafts, such as worm art, nest sculptures, and feather drawings. Specially made beak protectors are available.

MUSIC: Who doesn't like to shake a tail feather or two at a party? But music can also be a wonderful way to change your mood. Local area musicians teach you how to make a calming chant or upbeat tune the sound track of your life.

THE 5 STAGES OF ANGER

Anger is a part of life. Every bird feels it. But sometimes that anger takes over and does more than ruffle feathers—it is enough to make you want to pluck yourself (or others) bald! That is when you know you have a real anger problem. Below are the five stages of anger, based on scientific research and years of practice. Recognizing these stages in yourself and others will help diffuse any situation before you're at Stage 3 or beyond.

STAGE 1: IRRITATED

Sometimes something another bird says or does, or even the mood you wake up in, makes you irritated. This is pretty mild anger, so usually a few deep breaths or doing an activity you like turns your day around and changes your mood.

STAGE 2: ANNOYED

When other birds are rubbing your feathers the wrong way and you'd rather leave before you do something you'll regret, that's officially called annoyed. A little meditation or some yoga usually will return you to your normal happy bird state.

STAGE 3: REALLY ANGRY

When something or somebirdy makes you SO angry that you could scream, that's *really* angry. If you get to this stage, regular meditation and yoga won't necessarily work. You'll need the calming influence of a professional. Stop by the Infinity Acceptance Center as soon as possible.

STAGE 4: EXPLOSIVE

This is when you are so angry you feel you might actually explode! For most birds, this is as angry as they get. Multiple sessions at the Infinity Acceptance Center are strongly encouraged.

STAGE 5: SEEING RED

Red is so angry he actually gets a category all to himself! In all my years teaching at the Infinity Acceptance Center, I have never come across a bird more stubborn, more furious, or more rebellious. I hope that one day he can either let go of all that anger, or learn to channel it for good!

Zen Zone

Matilda's yoga classes are designed so that every bird can do them and feel his or her best. All that is required is an open mind and a willingness to learn! Here are just a few of the poses:

DANCER: This pose is best for stretching the whole body. It keeps you limber and loose so you can successfully face any obstacle that comes your way!

EAGLE: Spread those wings and reach for the sky! A noble pose for a noble bird.

HERON: Stand on one leg and maintain this pose as long as you can to achieve a state of Zen.

PEACOCK: A pose to warm up your lower body and allow you to show off your beautiful feathers!

WARRIOR: Channel your inner fighting spirit in this pose designed to show the beauty of strength.

MOUNTAIN: A quiet, still pose to channel and focus all your inner energy.

TREE: Solid, ancient, and unswaying, this pose roots you in the Now.

RABBIT: Hop along to peacefulness with this challenging pose that gets you close to the ground.

FISH: Flip your imaginary fins upstream and find yourself in an ocean of calm and peace.

KING PIGEON: Stand with your wings close to your body and move your neck backward and forward to clear your mind of all troubles.

DOWNWARD DUCK: One of my favorite poses! Feel the stretch from the tips of your feathers to the bottoms of your talons as you release all the stress and bad energy.

PRACTICE THESE ANY TIME YOU FEEL ANGRY OR STRESSED. AND TRY NOT TO GET ANGRIER OR MORE STRESSED. MATILDA ENDS EACH CLASS WITH A REMINDER THAT YOGA WILL LEAD STUDENTS INTO SOMETHING KNOWN AS A STATE OF BIRDVANA.

RIDING THE EMOTIONAL ROLLERCOASTER WITH MATILDA

More than anything, Matilda wants her students to get in touch with their emotional journey at the Center. She had them complete "emotion stories." With their consent, she is sharing the latest group's emotion stories. And because Matilda leads by example, her story is also available.

Life on Bird Island is _____ and _____. The island is _____ and filled with lots of _____ nature and _____ weather. Bird Village is our home, and we are all a _____ bird community. There are lots of _____ things to do and _____ things to see in Bird Village, and every bird treats one another with _____. Every day is a new chance to explore new _____ and share _____ with friends.

The best things about being part of a _____ bird community are _____, _____, and _____. There is a sense of _____ and _____ in Bird Village, and these lead to us being very _____ birds. There is no _____ on Bird Island, and no need for _____ and _____ in our community. Every bird should be a _____ bird!

Every bird needs friends, and the best kind of friends are those who _____. The qualities I bring to my friendships are _____, _____, and _____. They are part of what make me so _____! I am _____ and _____ to live on Bird Island!

Matilda's answers in order of blanks: wonderful, calm, an oasis, gorgeous, ideal, close-knit, exciting, beautiful, respect, ideas, special times, thriving, the harmony, the unconditional acceptance, the affection we have for one another, peace, joy, content, trouble, anger, negativity, happy, are supporting and nurturing, my calm energy, my wisdom, my passion, my effective, proud, grateful

103

RIDING THE EMOTIONAL ROLLERCOASTER WITH RED

Life on Bird Island is _____ and _____. The island is _____ and filled with lots of _____ nature and _____ weather. Bird Village is our home, and we are all a _____ bird community. There are lots of _____ things to do and _____ things to see in Bird Village, and every bird treats one another with _____. Every day is a new chance to explore new _____ and share _____ with friends.

The best things about being part of a _____ bird community are _____, _____, and _____. There is a sense of _____ and _____ in Bird Village, and these lead to us being very _____ birds. There is no _____ on Bird Island, and no need for _____ and _____ in our community. Every bird should be a _____ bird!

Every bird needs friends, and the best kind of friends are those who _____. The qualities I bring to my friendships are _____, _____, and _____. They are part of what make me so _____! I am _____ and _____ to live on Bird Island!

Red's answers in order of blanks: dull, slow, big, endless, repetitive, mindless, similar, the same never-ending cheerfulness, sources of anger, annoyances, clingy, nothing, nothing, sameness, uniformity, close-minded, adventure, difference, complication, complicated, know when to leave you alone, independence, honesty, ?, irritated, resigned, okay

CHUCK

Life on Bird Island is _____ and _____. The island is _____ and filled with lots of _____ nature and _____ weather. Bird Village is our home, and we are all a _____ bird community. There are lots of _____ things to do and _____ things to see in Bird Village, and every bird treats one another with _____. Every day is a new chance to explore new _____ and share _____ with friends.

The best things about being part of a _____ bird community are _____, _____, and _____. There is a sense of _____ and _____ in Bird Village, and these lead to us being very _____ birds. There is no _____ on Bird Island, and no need for _____ and _____ in our community. Every bird should be a _____ bird!

Every bird needs friends, and the best kind of friends are those who _____. The qualities I bring to my friendships are _____, _____, and _____. They are part of what make me so _____! I am _____ and _____ to live on Bird Island!

Chuck's answers in order of blanks: fun, exciting, a great big playground, beautiful, beautiful, happy, super-fun, familiarity, adventures, fun things, super-happy restaurants, museums, nightlife, calm, ease, easy, worry, safety helmets, traffic lights, super-fast, let you express yourself, speed, loyalty, making really good coffee, ME; super-happy, really like

RIDING THE EMOTIONAL ROLLERCOASTER WITH BOMB

Life on Bird Island is _____ and _____. The island is _____ and filled with lots of _____ nature and _____ weather. Bird Village is our home, and we are all a _____ bird community. There are lots of _____ things to do and _____ things to see in Bird Village, and every bird treats one another with _____. Every day is a new chance to explore new _____ and share _____ with friends.

The best things about being part of a _____ bird community are _____, _____, and _____. There is a sense of _____ and _____ in Bird Village, and these lead to us being very _____ birds. There is no _____ on Bird Island, and no need for _____ and _____ in our community. Every bird should be a _____ bird!

Every bird needs friends, and the best kind of friends are those who _____. The qualities I bring to my friendships are _____, _____, and _____. They are part of what make me so _____! I am _____ and _____ to live on Bird Island!

Bombs answers in order of blanks: good, birdy, Bird Island, big, nice, good, hellos, days, food, big, stuff, more stuff, even more stuff, birds, hatchlings, fluffy, pollution, dry cleaners, shoes, good, don't mind when you explode, being big, feathery, friendly, Bomb, a bird

109

POP QUIZ!

Let's Be Friends

Friends come in all shapes, sizes . . . and personalities. Take this quiz and see who just might be your new BFF (Best Feathered Friend)!

YOU ARE NATURALLY CALM AND EASYGOING. WHICH OF THESE SOUNDS MOST APPEALING TO YOU IN TERMS OF YOUR BEST FRIEND'S PERSONALITY?

A You want to spend your time with someone just as relaxed and calm.

B You want to hang out with someone who is a bit more outgoing but knows when to keep things cool.

C You want to be with someone who is always energetic and on the go!

D You want to be with someone who is actually fun once he or she stops being a bit cranky.

You want to relax at the end of the week with your best friend. What sounds like the most fun to you?

A Going over to your friend's place to paint, draw, and express yourself.

B Playing board games and eating pizza.

C Going to play miniature golf and baseball at the park.

D Just being left alone so you can relax and do your own thing.

When things are bad, what type of friend do you appreciate most?

A Someone who comes over to talk with you about your feelings and helps you feel better.

B Someone who is there for you to hang out with and take your mind off your problems.

C Someone who gets you to be active and forget your problems.

D Someone who leaves you alone so you can just be by yourself.

You and your best friend are planning a vacation together. What sounds like the best vacation to you?

A A trip to a yoga retreat to meditate and find your Zen.

B A trip to explore nature and go camping.

C A trip to an amusement park to see and do as much as possible!

D Just staying around the house and hanging out and watching TV.

How often do you want to see your best friend?

A A few times a week so that you can share your latest news.

B On the weekends so you both have lots to talk about.

C Every day!

D Only if we both feel like it.

YOU AND YOUR BEST FRIEND WANT TO THROW A PARTY. WHAT SOUNDS LIKE THE KIND OF PARTY YOU BOTH WOULD WANT TO HAVE?

A A small gathering of your closest friends to do something creative and make some fun crafts.

B A really nice group of friends to split lots of pizza and ice cream with, and play a few games.

C An adventure-themed party with LOTS of activities and games and food.

D We would never want to have a party. Who wants all those people around?!

IF YOU ANSWERED A TO MOST QUESTIONS,
Matilda is your best friend! Your best friend is like you: cool, calm, and collected.

IF YOU ANSWERED B TO MOST QUESTIONS,
Bomb is your best friend! You like to have fun with your best friend, but not go too crazy.

IF YOU ANSWERED C TO MOST QUESTIONS,
Chuck is your best friend! Your best friend likes to do things at full speed, and that's just perfect with you!

IF YOU ANSWERED D TO MOST QUESTIONS,
Red is your best friend! You and your best friend like to spend as much time apart as you do together. You both need a lot of alone time.

SECTION 4

PIGNORANCE IS BLISS

It wouldn't be a complete picture of Bird Island if I didn't tell you about the underbelly of life here. I mean, I do try to ignore it—or specifically, *them*. But to understand the current state of bird affairs, I'll have to discuss my least favorite subject: pigs.

There are these things called pigs, and they've crashed their ship on Bird Island. And get this, they're all green! I don't trust them. Not one bit. But will any bird listen to me? No. They're all, "We love our new green friends! We're going to welcome them into our city and homes without hesitation!" Who does that?! Especially when they have no problem dropping anchor on some poor, unsuspecting hut. Unforgivable, right? Because that's exactly what they did to my hut . . . without so much as an *I'm sorry*. I'm telling you, something smells fishy about these pigs, and I'm going to get to the bottom of it. By applying another of Red's Rules: *always keep your mfffph . . . umfff . . . pooof . . .*

Yes, well. Thank you, angry red guy with the eyebrows, for that . . . um, curiously interesting introduction. I am Leonard, ambassador to the pigs of Piggy Island.

I'd like to introduce you now to myself and my kin, and to show you the charms of our culture. I'm sure by this point you need a break from all those birds—fascinating as they may be, of course. Sit back, grab your favorite beverage, and prepare to be blown away by the wonderful world of the pigs! I believe that Angry Bird was about to share a rule, before he decided to join my friends for a quick drink. So instead, how about I make a suggestion? *Just chill out. Bliss is practically guaranteed when pigs are in charge.*

PIGGY ISLAND

Ah, Piggy Island! What can be said about Piggy Island? A lot, actually, and it's all good. Piggy Island is a *wonderful* place to live, full of happy, lively pigs and the most beautiful nature, weather, and scenery ever known to pigkind. It is nestled in the middle of the calm and clear ocean, not too far away from Bird Island. With every luxury and amenity a pig could want, there is not a more ideal place to live. Why, the island is nothing short of magnificent!

HARBOR

SLING SHOT

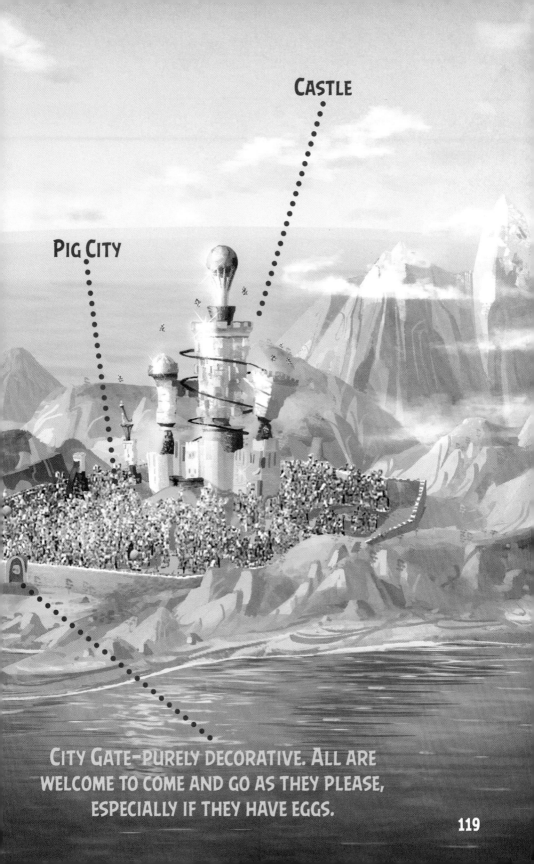

CASTLE

PIG CITY

CITY GATE—PURELY DECORATIVE. ALL ARE
WELCOME TO COME AND GO AS THEY PLEASE,
ESPECIALLY IF THEY HAVE EGGS.

PIG CITY

Pig City is the very heart of Piggy Island, where happy piggies live and where our generous—and handsome—King Pig rules. It is a city that represents the very best pig society can offer: dazzling inventions, towering structures, and lots of food, fireworks, and TNT! These last three are essential to everyday pig life. We are a creative, constructive culture, after all.

King Pig's castle lies at the center of Pig City, with all the other pigs living, working, and building all around the castle in an effort to make the city as appealing as possible. The sense of contentment and happiness in Pig City is directly related to the high quality of life on the island, as well as to the wide, er, wise rule of King Pig.

Pig Ship

The pig ship is a fine example of classic pig construction: durable, elegant, and packed with everything a pig might need for a voyage. There are a few minor flaws in the design—the ramp only works about 50 percent of the time—but all in all, it is a marvel. Plus, the pigs are working on a bold solution.

This vessel can house more than one hundred pigs, a room full of trampolines, countless copies of our favorite books, and an ample wardrobe of cowboy outfits. These are all essential items for the Bird Island mission—allowing the pigs to share their sophisticated culture *and* ensuring a comfortable trip.

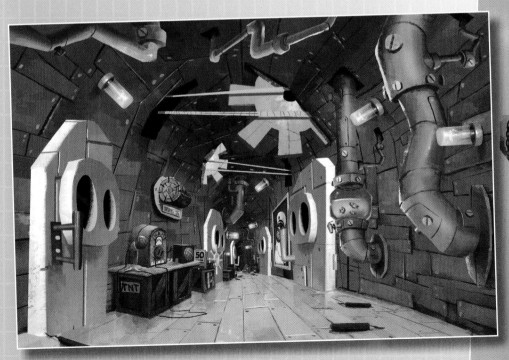

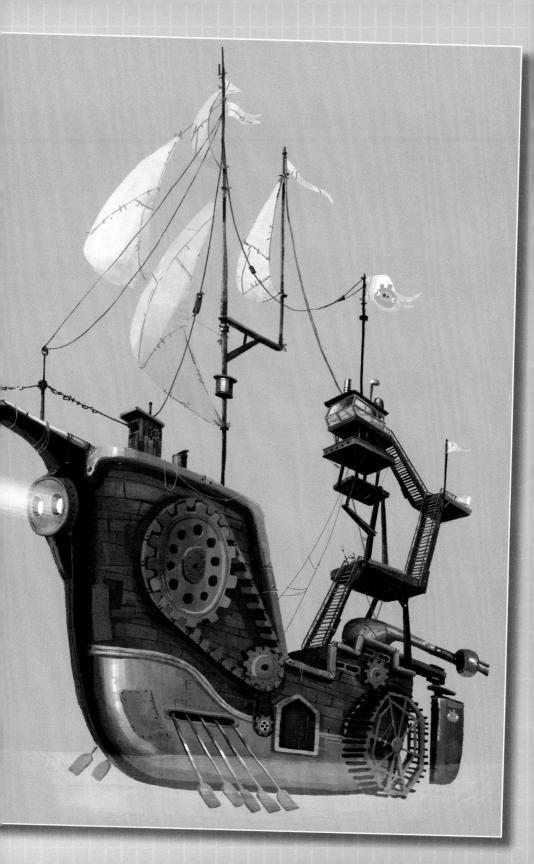

We pigs love to put on a cowboy show. Indeed, some of my trusty cousins only feel truly happy when dressed in leather chaps and line dancing to the strum of a banjo. That's why we always have a closet full of tassels and Stetsons at the ready. Rawhide!

COSTUME CLOSET

TNT ROOM

THE GIFT THAT KEEPS ON GIVING

Being an ambassador of Piggy Island, I would never think of arriving on Bird Island empty-handed. The pigs and I presented the lovely birds with several pig-made gifts to make their lives easier and more convenient—not to mention more enjoyable. The largest and most memorable (as well as heaviest) of these gifts is called the slingshot.

Why waste time and precious energy carrying things when they can be placed on this slingshot, pulled back, and released.

The sense of well-being and accomplishment is guaranteed as each item hurtles toward its destination in a graceful arc. There's nothing like genuine pig-made efficiency to make the day a little easier. The slingshot is even large enough to accommodate the birds themselves, which will make their getting around their island even faster. We give the birds gifts like these to keep them happy. Pigs are generous like that. What could possibly go wrong?

LEONARD

I am the first to admit that I am just a humble pig. I want nothing more than to be friends with the birds—a modest goal for a modest pig.

My job is a cross between an ambassador and a salespig—spreading the word about the great and beautiful culture of Piggy Island, and how that culture should be forced on—er, shared with other cultures to promote exchange and growth. It's why we pigs came to Bird Island: a rich, savory, delicious, uh, chance to exchange ideas. I firmly believe that the best way to accomplish this is by surrendering complete trust and control. It's the best way for the pig program to work. What could go wrong?

ALL ABOUT LEONARD

OCCUPATION: Master of Ceremonies and leader of the pigs' voyage to Bird Island.

FAVORITE COLOR: Green. And soft white, like the color of those lovely eggs I see all around Bird Village.

FAVORITE BOOK: I prefer the classics, especially *Huckleberry Pig* and *Piglas Shrugged*.

SPECIAL SKILLS: Line dancing, yodeling.

HOBBIES: Fine dining, hosting parties, politics, power.

FAVORITE PLACE ON PIGGY ISLAND: King Pig's castle is a truly magnificent palace fit for a beloved monarch.

BEST FRIEND: I think of every pig as a friend, but, truth be told, it's hard for me to find an equal.

GREATEST WISH: To unite the pig and eggs . . . I mean pigs and *birds* in a giant celebration of mutual respect and love!

BIGGEST FEAR: Not achieving my greatest wish!

WHAT MAKES YOU HAPPY? The chance to use my diplomacy skills to forge new and lasting relationships.

WHAT MAKES YOU ANGRY? Those who do not cooperate.

MOTTO: Power is a many-splendored thing.

ROSS

Ross is my trusted associate and assistant. He helps make sure that diplomatic missions go smoothly. He's a simple, hard-working, and honest fellow, especially when it comes to my cares and concerns. Attentive to every last detail, Ross will go out of his way to make me happy. Did I mention he is simple? Because he is. Very simple. Simple is probably his middle name.

ALL ABOUT ROSS

OCCUPATION: First Officer and Assistant Pig.

FAVORITE COLOR: Green.

FAVORITE BOOK: *Tinker, Tailor, Soldier, Pig.*

SPECIAL SKILLS: I'm very good at assisting and first-officing.

HOBBIES: Whatever Leonard tells me to enjoy, especially sewing costumes.

FAVORITE PLACE ON PIGGY ISLAND: My workroom, where I can tinker and create new constructions.

BEST FRIEND: Leonard, of course, and all other pigs.

GREATEST WISH: Leonard's endless happiness.

BIGGEST FEAR: Same as Leonard—whatever it is.

WHAT MAKES YOU HAPPY? If Leonard is happy, I'm happy.

WHAT MAKES YOU ANGRY? Not getting food.

MOTTO: Make Leonard happy.

THE PIGS

The pigs are honest, decent, kind, and incredibly dim-witted folk. If properly guided by some brilliant pig, for instance, they can do marvelous things. They like to build, sew costumes, dance, party, and eat, and that's pretty much it. Aren't they so gosh darn adorable?

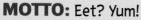

ALL ABOUT THE PIGS

OCCUPATION: Pigz.

FAVORITE COLOR: Greeen.

FAVORITE BOOK: What iz book?

SPECIAL SKILLS: Building. Smyling. Eeting.

HOBBIES: Awl of it.

FAVORITE PLACE ON PIGGY ISLAND: Pig Citee.

BEST FRIEND: Eech other!

GREATEST WISH: Moar food!

BIGGEST FEAR: Not enuf food!

WHAT MAKES YOU HAPPY? Food! Billding! Explosives!

WHAT MAKES YOU ANGRY? Angreee?

MOTTO: Eet? Yum!

PIG CONSTRUCTION

The constructions and dwellings on Piggy Island are some of the most stunning examples of the pigs' ingenuity. Built by hand, each and every construction is guaranteed to last for as long as gravity allows. I often remind old and new friends that it's hard not to view Piggy Island as one of the most magical places anywhere. It's not like I'm biased or anything. Here, I'll let the pigs show you.

PIGGY TOWERS

GREAT VIEWS!
COMING SOON:
STAIRS

TNT TERRACE

AVOID WHEN WINDY, OR RAINY, OR SNOWY, OR SUNNY . . . JUST AVOID.

BALLOON COURT

ALMOST AS HIGH
AS THE KING'S CASTLE!

PARTY-LIKE
ATMOSPHERE 24/7

Construction Place

Rotating Crane

Handy stash of TNT

COIL RIDGE

BOUNCY FOUNDATION

SUPER-STRONG ROPE

HALF-PIPE POINTE SKATERS' RAMP

FOR SALE:
VERY REASONABLY PRICED!

ROAD HOGS

The pigs may be simple, but their vehicles sure aren't! They spend a lot of time customizing their vehicles, because stylish and multifunctional make for a smooth ride whether they're low on the ground or high in the sky.

HOGGER

SIDE-HOG MINIROCKET

TRAINING WHEELS

SMASHER

SMASHY THING!

SMASHY THING
START BUTTON

The Vroomliner comes in especially handy when there are planes to fly, but you still want to travel from the tops of tall buildings. It doesn't go very far, but it feels funny when your tummy drops from under you! Whee!

UMBRELLA (MAKES LANDINGS LESS BOUNCY)

VROOM JET

VROOMLINER

BLASTER

WATER
BLASTER

FASTER
BLASTER

The Blaster is designed for full-on bird destruction, er . . . having a grand ole time cooling down pigs on a hot summer's day! Yes, that's all. Oh! And it goes fast, too!

The crème de la crème of porcine planery—the Turbo goes from oink to 60 before you can say "bacon"! Just make sure you don't touch any of the buttons or it might fall apart. . . .

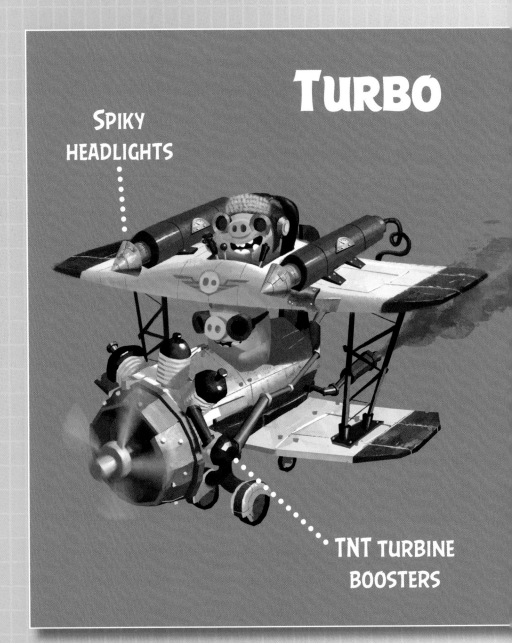

TURBO

SPIKY
HEADLIGHTS

TNT TURBINE
BOOSTERS

PLUNGEMOBILE

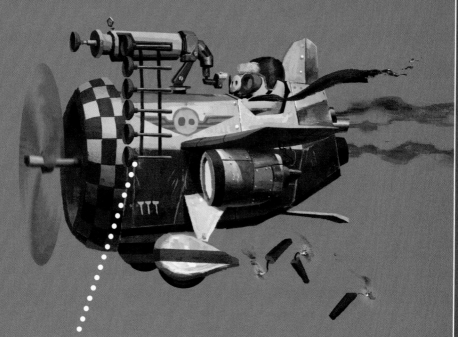

PROPEL-O-PLUNGERS

TNT, telescopic sights, plungers . . . this flying machine has everything you need for, er . . . a quiet, peaceful flight over Bird Island with our feathered friends!

THE CASTLE

The kind and brilliant King lives in a castle perched on the highest point of Piggy Island. It's important for him to be able to see all points of his kingdom. And it's even more important that all the pigs *look up to him* every moment of every day.

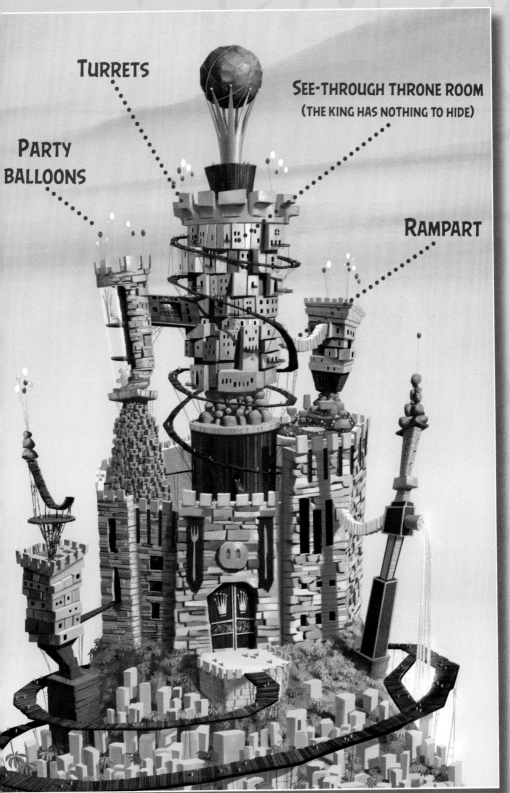

TURRETS

SEE-THROUGH THRONE ROOM
(THE KING HAS NOTHING TO HIDE)

PARTY
BALLOONS

RAMPART

147

THE THRONE ROOM

148

PIG PARTY TIPS

Throwing a party pig-style is about as simple as the pigs. Here are a few *very easy-to-follow* steps that will ensure a successful blowout.

2

SET THE MOOD.
START THE PARTY
WITH A GROUP
YODEL.

4
MAKE SURE THE
ENTERTAINMENT IS
TOP-NOTCH. GRAB
YOUR COWBOY HAT
AND BOOTS, FOR SOME
SPIGTACULAR LINE
DANCING.

POP QUIZ!

Piggy Edition

Have you soaked up enough pig culture yet to proclaim yourself a pig connoisseur? I would love to see how you do on this quiz about my beloved pigs.

1. TRUE OR FALSE:

Bird Island and Piggy Island are located directly next to each other.

2. THE PIGS ARE LED BY A WISE AND WONDERFUL KING.

Where does this king live?

3. OUR PIG SHIP IS STOCKED WITH THREE IMPORTANT THINGS FOR ALL OUR JOURNEYS:

A TNT, toothpaste, and trampolines

B Copies of *Fifty Shades of Green*, trampolines, and cowboy outfits

C Cowboy outfits, fresh flowers, and soda pop

D Trampolines, TNT, and lemons

4. TRUE OR FALSE:

The pigs tend to be a sad, quiet bunch that keep to themselves.

5. WHAT IS EVERY PIG'S FAVORITE COLOR?

6. WHAT IS OUR PURPOSE IN VISITING BIRD ISLAND?

A To look at new land to expand our Pig kingdom

B To escape from our overcrowded island and seek a new home

C To make friends with our bird neighbors and encourage working together

D To vacation for a few months

7. WHICH PIG INVENTION DID WE GIVE AS A GIFT TO THE BIRDS?

8. WHAT IS THE NAME OF MY ASSISTANT AND FIRST OFFICER?

9. WHAT DO I LIKE ALL MY FRIENDS TO CALL ME?

10. TRUE OR FALSE:

Piggy Island is the greatest place to live.

And . . . I'm back. Wow, that was a LOT of information and a LOT of one pig's ego. Like I said, something about that pig rubs my feathers the wrong way. I'm going to keep an eye on him while he and his "friends" are here. No one is going to try to ruin my home while I'm around!

Wait one second! Did I just call Bird Island my home and feel really proud instead of really angry? Am I actually feeling *happy* to live here? Life on Bird Island is pretty good, but maybe all this talking has deprived my bird brain of oxygen. This anger-management stuff can't possibly be working, can it?

So remember, that last rule I had for you? Here goes: *always keep your eyes open because you never know what you might find—* it might be happiness . . . or new friends . . . or maybe there's a group of suspicious pigs that needs investigating. Whatever it is, Bird Island has it all.